About the Book

It was the summer of 1777, and the small town of Bennington, Vermont, was roused in the middle of the night. The British redcoats had just captured Fort Ticonderoga. Now they were on their way to take the supplies stored near Bennington!

Nine-year-old Aaron Robinson could not contain his excitement. He pictured himself bravely running through the lines with messages for the generals, or heroically guarding his grandfather's tavern, or even taking part in a battle with the Green Mountain Boys. But whenever he eagerly offered his services, he was told to help his grandfather bake bread for the soldiers instead—pretty tame work for a boy who could shoot a blackbird at 100 paces.

Patricia Lee Gauch tells this Revolutionary War tale based on a true story with simplicity and humor, and illustrations by Margot Tomes bring the period and characters to life for young history fans.

AARON
AND THE
GREEN MOUNTAIN BOYS

by

PATRICIA LEE GAUCH

PICTURES by

MARGOT TOMES

COWARD, McCANN & GEOGHEGAN, INC.
NEW YORK

About the Author

PATRICIA LEE GAUCH grew up near Detroit, Michigan, and has since lived in Kentucky, Illinois, Ohio, and New York. She and her husband, Ronald, now live with their three young children in Basking Ridge, New Jersey.

Formerly a journalist for the La Grange *Citizen* and Louisville *Courier-Journal*, Mrs. Gauch has always been interested in history. In recent years her research has taken her and her whole family all over New England to forts, to old houses, and battlegrounds. *Aaron and the Green Mountain Boys* is her first history for young readers. She is also the author of *A Secret House*, illustrated by Margot Tomes.

About the Artist

MARGOT TOMES was born in Yonkers, New York, and was graduated from Pratt Institute.

She has illustrated several children's books such as *Joe and the Talking Christmas Tree* by Dale Fife, *A Secret House* by Patricia Lee Gauch, and *Plenty for Three* by Liesel Moak Skorpen. In addition to her work as an illustrator, she is a textile designer.

Miss Tomes lives and works in New York City.

Library of Congress Catalog Card Number: 70-169246

PRINTED IN THE UNITED STATES OF AMERICA
06209

For Ronald

CONTENTS

Chapter 1
Something's Up!

It was a summer night in 1777.

Aaron heard a door squeak shut.

He jumped out of bed

and ran to the window.

Below, Pa was swinging his lantern

as he hurried down the lane.

Other lanterns dotted the night.

It was the Green Mountain Boys!

Something was up!

"It's the war, I know it!"
Aaron pulled on his pants.
He lived in Bennington,
a little village in the Green
Mountains of Vermont.
The British king ruled it
and all America.
A lot of Americans didn't think
the king ruled fairly.
They had gone to war to stop him.

Once in Aaron's own grandpa's
tavern he had heard villagers shout,
"We'll have freedom from Britain
or die!"
The fighters were called
Green Mountain Boys.

But they hadn't needed to fight —
not since they had won Fort
Ticonderoga.
The fort could keep
any Britishers away!
But then ... why the rush
in the middle of the night?

Aaron sneaked down the stairs
and ran to Grandpa's tavern.
That was the town's meeting place.
He crept into the kitchen
and opened the hall door a crack.

A colonel was standing on a table.
"The British have captured
the fort! And they know horses
and wagons and cattle
are stored near Bennington.
Redcoats are on their way here now!"
Redcoats were enemy soldiers!
"But we've only a hundred
Green Mountain Boys here,"
someone shouted.
"I've sent to New Hampshire for
help," the colonel said.
"But until it comes, we must
be ready for anything!"

"I'll be ready!" Aaron said out loud.
He turned to see
Grandpa scowling behind him.
"The Boys need help," he offered.
"And I need help washing all
these extra mugs," Grandpa said.

Chapter 2
Aaron Gets an Ax

Some Green Mountain Boys started

right out to look for redcoats.

Some stayed in town to wait for help.

Pa stayed.

One day he climbed up on a fence.

"The soldiers from New Hampshire

are coming!" he shouted.

Aaron climbed up, too.

"They don't look much

like soldiers to me," he said.

"They look like farmers."

But at the tavern Aaron saw a
general who looked like a general.
General John Stark.
He served him stew.

He heard him say, "The British
are only two towns away!
I'll need every man who can
hold a gun, and I'll need bread
to feed an army."

"And you'll need the rest of
the Green Mountain Boys back here!
I'll ride to get them," Pa said.
"I'll get the bread," said Grandpa.

Aaron caught Pa at the door.

"I'll go with you, Pa!"

"No, son."

"Then I'll go with the general."

"No, Aaron."

"Then I'll—"

"Then . . . you'll stay home
and help your ma!"

In the next hour
everyone seemed to have
something to do —
except Aaron.

The men followed
the general out of town.
Women bolted their doors.
Some hid their children in cellars.

And Grandpa sat down

and started to count.

"Let's see ... there are about

fifteen hundred men.

Five men will eat

one loaf in one day.

In one day fifteen hundred men

will eat" — he paused —

"three hundred loaves!

But I have only two hands.

How can I chop the wood

and mix the batter and bake the

bread to feed fifteen hundred?"

"I'll get help, Father," Ma said.

"And I can mix a good batter myself!"

"I'll help, too, Grandpa,"
Aaron said. "I can guard the tavern
or take messages to the general or —"

"How about

chopping the wood

to keep the ovens hot?"

"Yes, I could do that, I guess,"

Aaron said weakly.

It wasn't what he had in mind.

Chapter 3
Bread! Bread! Bread!

That same hour Aaron started
to chop. Whack. Whack. Whack.
And the pile grew higher

and higher

and higher.

By afternoon the oven fires
were roaring. By nightfall Aaron
smelled the bread baking.
By the time he went to bed

Ma and Grandpa were stacking
the loaves on the table,
the shelves, the windowsills.

But Aaron wasn't thinking
about bread. He was thinking,
"What a place to be, stuck in bed!"
All night he kept listening
for the rumble of cannons
or the shots of guns. But all
he heard were the ch-r-r-r-p
of crickets and the b-a-r-r-up
of bullfrogs. At dawn he ran

to meet the bread wagon.

"Sir," he said to the soldiers,

"has the battle begun?"

"Begun? The rest of the Green

Mountain Boys have not even come!

And the redcoats are only

one town away!"

I'll ride for the Boys," Aaron said.

"Your pa's already done that!"

Grandpa said.

"Maybe they're in trouble."

"And maybe they just have

a long way to march!"

"Well, then I'll go to the general.

He needs more men!" Aaron said.

"And I need more work

and less talk!" said Grandpa,

and he handed Aaron the ax.

"Bread!" Aaron scoffed.

In the middle of that night

Aaron heard rumbling.

But not cannon.

It was thunder.

Then it began to rain,

first in sprinkles,

then in bucketfuls.

The next day the bread wagon

didn't come and didn't come.

Grandpa started to pace.

Finally he said,

"Hitch the horses.

We'll deliver the bread."

The two drove off in a pelting rain,

past the church, down the hill.

The road was flowing like a stream.

They finally saw the camp.

It looked like

a soggy patchwork quilt.

The general met Grandpa.

"Have you seen the rest of

the Green Mountain Boys?"

"No," Grandpa said. "Haven't you?"

"No. It must be this blasted weather!

The Boys can't get through,

our guns won't fire,

and the enemy is digging in

for battle just up the river!

Not only redcoats,

but troops with swords and cannon."

The general shook his head.

"Well, we can wait no longer.

If the sun shines tomorrow,

we'll attack with or without

those Green Mountain Boys."

Aaron poked Grandpa.

"I'll stay!" he whispered.

"Tell the general I can shoot

a blackbird at one hundred paces."

"Pardon?" the general asked.

"Nothing, sir. The boy wants
to *shoot* home and do some
chopping before bed."

The general smiled. "Good boy.
Keep the bread coming!"

Aaron tried to smile back.

Bread! Bread! Bread!

Chapter 4
A Surprise by Night

On the way home the rain streamed
into Aaron's eyes. The horses
slipped and stumbled.
By the time he saw the lighted
windows Aaron was thinking
of one thing — a warm, dry bed.

But when he opened the door,

he saw —

Pa and Green Mountain Boys
and some new fighters, too —
all dripping wet!
"Pa!" Aaron flung himself
at his father.
"We've marched all day
to reach the general,
but we can't go another step!
Our guns are drenched and...."
Pa stumbled to a chair.
"Pa, you look awful!" Aaron said.
"We're hungry," Pa said.
"We've hardly had a bite
to eat for two days."

Grandpa drew him closer
to the hearth. "Come.
We have a roaring fire to
dry your guns."
"And there's bread aplenty," Ma said.
She had been working all day.

The men stacked their guns
around the fire.
Aaron helped Ma bring in
the plates of warm bread
and pails of milk.

Pa and the others grabbed
the loaves and tore them apart.
They stuffed the bread
into their mouths.
"They eat bread like it was
a Thanksgiving turkey," Aaron said.

"They're hungry," Grandpa told him.

"I guess I've never been

that hungry," Aaron said.

"Now we can fight a battle!"
Pa said, stretching himself.

All night the men dried their guns,
Ma and Grandpa baked,
and Aaron kept the fires hot.
This time he didn't mind a bit.

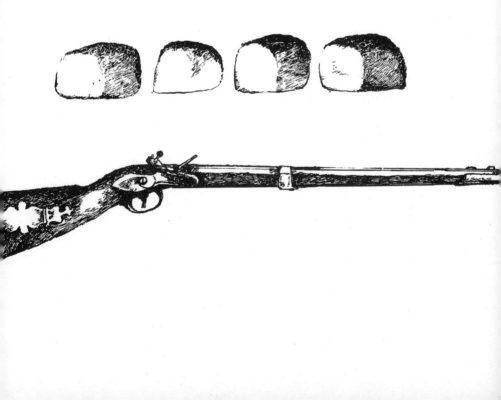

Chapter 5
A Race to the River

In the morning the sun shone.
The Green Mountain Boys raced
the wagons toward the river camp.
Aaron showed them the way,
but the road was muddy.
"I hope we make it in time,"
Aaron said.

But when they got there,
the camp was deserted.
Suddenly, the sound of cannon
thundered over the woods.
"We're too late!" Pa shouted.

But a farmer ran up.

"Quick! More redcoats have come!

The general needs help!"

"Giddyap!" Pa hollered.

The horses flew through the woods,

over sticks, and ruts, and puddles.

The thunder grew closer

baroom

and closer

BAROOM

and closer

B-A-R-O-O-M

"I see them!" someone shouted.

The Boys tore through the woods.

"Aiiiiiiiiyyyeeeee!" they shouted.

"Stay with the horses, Aaron,"

Pa yelled.

That wasn't so easy.

Flames were leaping into the air.

Puffs of smoke were everywhere.

The British cannon kept exploding

over and over.

Then for a moment the smoke cleared.

The Boys had reached the general!

"Thank the Lord, you've come!"

the general shouted.

Now all the Green Mountain Boys
and all the farmers surged together
against the enemy.

They fought hand to hand.
Aaron could see the enemy
swords flashing.
Even the swords couldn't
stop the Americans.
"They look like farmers,
but they're soldiers all right,"
Aaron thought.

And soon the air grew still.
The thunder stopped,
and through the smoke Aaron saw
the Green Mountain Boys
and the general and the farmers
bringing in prisoners.
The Americans had won!

The stars shone
as the wagon rattled
toward Bennington.
"I'll never forget tonight, Pa!"
Aaron said.
"None of us will,"
said Aaron's father.
"And none of us will forget
last night either."
Aaron yawned.
That reminded him.
He hadn't slept for more than a day.
He guessed now was a good time
to start catching up.

Epilogue

In Bennington in 1777 there was a real boy named Aaron. Aaron Robinson. He was indeed the tavernkeeper's grandson, and the story goes, "He chopped the wood" so that his mother and other village women could bake the bread that fed the patriot army.

Whether Aaron really made it to the battle, we do not know. But we do know that the bread the villagers made and their fires enabled the Green Mountain Boys to get to the battle scene with full stomachs and dried rifles just in the nick of time.

And we know that ten of Aaron Robinson's uncles fought in the battle, reason enough for a nine-year-old boy to want to do his part, too, in the American fight for freedom.